Five reasons why we think you'll love this book!

Winnie and Wilbur
HAPPY BIRTHDAY, WINNIE

Winnie's having a party . . . and you're invited!

You get to meet Winnie's family.

There is so much to spot in every picture.

Contains a lot of cake!

You can take the Winnie and Wilbur challenge: how many yellow bows can you find?

Freya

Anushka

Maggie

Bailey

Johannes

Molly

Ashley

Amber

Jun-Yeong

Pablo

Matilda

Marwin

Hasan

Rebecca

Thank you to all these schools for helping with the endpapers:

St Barnabas Primary School, Oxford; St Ebbe's Primary School, Oxford; Marcham Primary School, Abingdon; St Michael's C.E. Aided Primary School, Oxford; St Bede's RC Primary School, Jarrow; The Western Academy, Beijing, China; John King School, Pinxton; Neston Primary School, Neston; Star of the Sea RC Primary School, Whitley Bay; José Jorge Letria Primary School, Cascais, Portugal; Dunmore Primary School, Abingdon; Özel Bahçeşehir İlköğretim Okulu, Istanbul, Turkey; the International School of Amsterdam, the Netherlands; Princethorpe Infant School, Birmingham.

For Eve, who has given so many
lovely parties—V.T.

For our daughter Zoë who is the
same age as Winnie—K.P.

OXFORD
UNIVERSITY PRESS

Great Clarendon Street, Oxford OX2 6DP

Oxford University Press is a department of the University of Oxford. It furthers the University's objective of excellence in research, scholarship, and education by publishing worldwide. Oxford is a registered trade mark of Oxford University Press in the UK and in certain other countries

Text copyright © Valerie Thomas 2007
Illustrations copyright © Korky Paul 2007, 2016
The moral rights of the author and artist
have been asserted

Database right Oxford University Press (maker)

First published as *Happy Birthday, Winnie!* in 2007
This edition first published in 2016

British Library Cataloguing in Publication Data available

ISBN: 978-0-19-274824-9 (paperback)
ISBN: 978-0-19-274917-8 (paperback and CD)

10 9 8 7 6 5 4 3 2 1

Printed in China

Paper used in the production of this book is a natural, recyclable product made from wood grown in sustainable forests. The manufacturing process conforms to the environmental regulations of the country of origin

www.winnieandwilbur.com

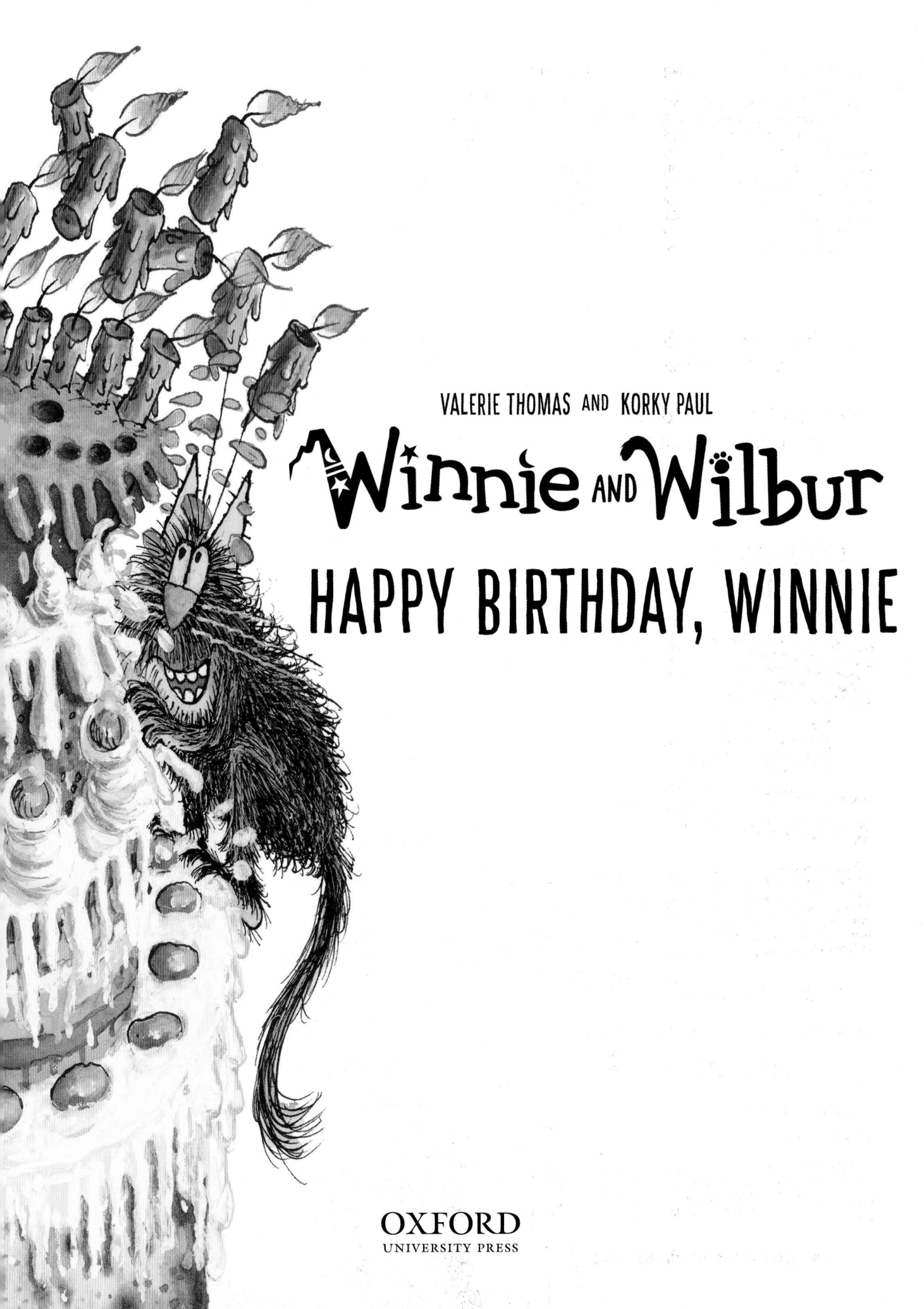

VALERIE THOMAS AND KORKY PAUL

Winnie and Wilbur

HAPPY BIRTHDAY, WINNIE

OXFORD
UNIVERSITY PRESS

When Winnie the Witch turned over the
page on her calendar, she saw a big red
circle around Friday the thirteenth.

'That's my birthday!' she said.
'I'll have a party this year, Wilbur.'
'Purr,' said Wilbur. He loved parties.

'What kind of party?' Winnie wondered.
'I know, a garden party.'

On Monday Winnie wrote out the invitations
and sent them by Winni-e-mail.
She invited . . .

Aunty Alice,
Uncle Owen,
her three sisters Wanda, Wilma, and Wendy,
all of her friends,
and Cousin Cuthbert.

On Tuesday she made herself a party dress,
and a matching bow for Wilbur.
'Purr,' said Wilbur. I look lovely, he thought.

On Wednesday Winnie made
lots and lots of food.
Wilbur helped.

WEDNESDAY 11th

Thursday was the day to get the garden ready.
Winnie went outside. It looked rather scruffy.
Then Winnie had a very good idea.
She took out her wand, waved it, shouted,

'Abracadabra!'

. . . and the garden was ready for the party.
'That was easy,' Winnie said.

'Now what else? Oh yes, I need a surprise.
A good party always has a surprise.
I'll have to think about that.'

Friday the thirteenth was a lovely sunny day,
which was lucky.

At two o'clock Winnie's guests arrived.
'Happy birthday, Winnie,' they shouted,
and they piled up the presents on the lawn.

Wanda, Wilma, and Wendy gave
Winnie a magic carpet.
She'd always wanted one of those.

Uncle Owen gave her
a bat in a cage.
She'd never wanted one of those.

Aunty Alice gave her a Book
of Special Spells,

and there was a magic trumpet
from Cousin Cuthbert.

'Let's play some games!' Winnie said.
First they played musical broomsticks.
That was fun, but there was a lot of pushing.
Uncle Owen pushed Aunty Alice into a prickle bush. **Ouch!**

Cousin Cuthbert bounced off a broomstick and landed in the fountain. So they let him win.

'Now we'll have a treasure hunt,' said Winnie.

Uncle Owen looked in the maze, and got lost.

Wilma looked in the bat's cage, and the bat flew away.

Wendy looked in the bouncy castle.
Bang!

Wanda found the treasure, but she had some help.

'The next game is hide-and-seek,' Winnie shouted.
But there was so much noise nobody heard her.

So Winnie picked up her new magic trumpet.
Toot, toot, toot,
Winnie tootled . . .

and **everybody** disappeared.
Winnie was surprised.

Then she was cross.
Where had they gone?

Winnie looked
in the maze.
Nobody.

She looked in the
bat's cage.
Nothing.

She looked in the
bouncy castle.
Nobody.

'Blithering broomsticks!' Winnie said.
'Who will eat all my lovely food?'

Then Winnie saw a label on the trumpet.

IMPORTANT:
to make people disappear, toot three times
to make them come back, stand on your head
and toot three times

So Winnie stood on her head.
Toot, toot, toot,
she tootled . . .

and everybody came back, feeling hungry.
They ate up all the food.

'And now it's time for the surprise,' said Winnie.
She opened her new Book of Special Spells.
'Shut your eyes and think about your
favourite cake!' she said.

Everybody shut their eyes.
Aunty Alice thought about chocolate cake.
Uncle Owen thought about fruit cake.
Cousin Cuthbert thought about rainbow cake.
Wilbur thought about cheesecake.
He loved cheesecake.

Then Winnie the Witch shut her eyes,
turned around three times, stamped her foot,
waved her wand, and shouted,

'Abracadabra!'

... and there was the biggest birthday cake
in the whole world,
with candles on the top.

There was a layer of chocolate cake,
a layer of fruit cake,
a layer of rainbow cake,
a layer of cheesecake.
There was strawberry shortcake,
ginger sponge cake,
orange cake,
Black Forest cake.

'How will you blow out the candles?'
asked Cousin Cuthbert.
'That's easy,' Winnie said . . .

and she rode on her magic carpet to the top of the cake.
Puff, puff, puuffffffff!

'Ha ha ha,' laughed Winnie.
'This party is such fun, Wilbur!
I'm a very lucky witch.'

Wilbur didn't say anything.
His mouth was full of cheesecake.
What a lucky black cat!

Happy Birthday to you!

Bethany

Katia

Eun-Jae

Kathleen

Ji-Eun

Fraser

Ka Keung

Selin

Selin

Olivia

A note for grown-ups

Oxford Owl is a FREE and easy-to-use website packed with support and advice about everything to do with reading.

Informative videos

Hints, tips and fun activities

Top tips from top writers for reading with your child

Help with choosing picture books

For this expert advice and much, much more about how children learn to read and how to keep them reading ...

LOOK
for Oxford Owl
www.oxfordowl.co.uk